In the desert long ago, Snake had no rattle on the end of his tail. He just slid silently across the desert floor. He was afraid of many things. This tale tells how he got his rattle...and his courage.

All the animals loved to play desert ball. Snake liked to play, but he was very, very shy. He was always picked last to be on a desert ball team. Snake couldn't move across the field as fast as Hare. He couldn't catch as well as Coyote. And he certainly couldn't fly like Hawk.

During games, Snake always tried to catch the ball. He usually could not reach it. The ball would roll right past him. Snake would slide after it. He would put the ball in his mouth and then try to throw it. Every single time, the ball would fall out of his mouth. It was hard for Snake to play desert ball!

The animals played desert ball as often as they could. They would only stop for one reason. All play ended on the spot when the wild horses came. The horses would storm out of the hills and run right through the desert ball field. Their hooves kicked rocks high into the air. Everyone ran to hide when they came.

During a desert ball game one day, the animals heard a thundering sound. The wild horses were coming! It looked like there were hundreds and hundreds of them. Everyone ran to hide. But snake was too scared to move. All he could do was twitch his tail back and forth.

The wild horses charged across the
desert. Rocks flew through the air as
the horses raced toward the field. Snake
watched as they came closer and closer.
He wished he could move, but he could
not budge.

Soon the wild horses were all around Snake. He tried not to be so shy. Snake hissed at them, but no sound came out. Each time he hissed, he got a mouthful of rocks instead. He wanted to spit the rocks out, but all he could do was swallow.

He had gulped down so many rocks
that he could feel his stomach getting
very heavy. But snake did not give up.
He kept trying to hiss at the horses.

"Look out!" the animals yelled at Snake. At the last minute, Hawk came to the rescue. He dropped down from the sky and grabbed Snake. Then Hawk set him safely down.

All the animals made fun of Snake because he was so afraid. "Scaredy snake!" giggled Coyote.

Poor Snake felt very foolish.

Snake slowly slithered away and hid beside a large rock. All the rocks he had swallowed made his stomach hurt.

The next day, Roadrunner visited Snake. From the rumble in Roadrunner's stomach, Snake knew she was very hungry! Snake did not want to be her lunch.

"Is that you there, Snake?" asked Roadrunner. "We're going to play desert ball, and everyone's asking for you. Come on out!"

Of course, Snake knew this wasn't true. Roadrunner was trying to trick him into being her next meal. Snake was scared.

Roadrunner tried and tried to trick Snake into coming out. Snake got so frightened that his tail began to shake. Each time it shook, he heard a click and clack sound.

"What's that sound?" Roadrunner asked Snake.

Snake said, "I don't know. I've never heard it before."

Roadrunner thought it was the wild horses coming, so she ran to hide.

Snake sighed. Roadrunner finally had gone away. Snake did not know what had made that strange new sound. Each time he moved, he heard that click and clack again. Snake wondered where it was coming from.

Then the sound of thunder filled the air. That could only be the wild horses!

"Oh, no!" hissed Snake, just as the horses were coming. Snake could not move. His tail shook back and forth making a click, clack, click, clack sound. Snake grew more frightened. His tail shook harder. The noise it made sounded just like a rattle.

Snake's own tail was making the rattling sound. The rocks he swallowed had gone down to the very tip of his tail.

The wild horses slowed down and looked around. Snake couldn't believe it. The horses looked afraid. Could they be afraid of him?

It seemed strange to Snake that the wild horses were afraid. After all, they were the bravest animals in the whole desert. They didn't fear anything or anyone. The other animals were always scared of them. Now the wild horses were frightened by Snake.

Snake's rattling got so loud that the horses jumped up into the air. They began running in circles. They got more and more frightened. Snake kept right on rattling. Then the wild horses turned and ran away as fast as they could. Snake had done it! He had scared them off all by himself!

The other animals ran toward Snake. Hare said, "I can't believe it. You scared away the wild horses!"

"You were very brave," said Hawk.

"Your tail sounds like it has a rattle on the end of it," said Coyote.

Snake was a hero. The animals talked about how brave he was. Snake was proud of himself. He had faced those wild horses with courage. Then all the other animals began to call him "Rattlesnake."

It's a good thing that Snake swallowed all those rocks. Now he could take care of himself just by rattling his tail. He could also play desert ball much better. His new tail helped him hit the ball farther than any other animal. All the animals wanted Rattlesnake on their team!

Now the animals play desert ball as much as they like. If they hear the horses coming, they just ask Rattlesnake to rattle his tail. He faces the horses and shakes his tail. The rattle scares the wild horses away every time.

Ever since that day, all Rattlesnakes have a rattle on the end of their tail. And they have lots of courage, too.